I0538133

How Was Your Day Mom?

Rachel Stubbs

Illustrated by Kelly Kimble

Little Books of Love, LLC

This Book Belongs To:

_____

Copyright © 2014 by Rachel N. Stubbs
All rights reserved.
This book or any portion thereof
may not be reproduced or used in
any manner whatsoever
without the express written
permission of the publisher
except for the use of brief quotations
in a book review.

Printed in the United States of America

First Printing, 2014

ISBN 978-0-692-25129-4

Little Books of Love LLC
143 Forshaw Drive
Stockbridge, GA 30281 www.littlebooksoflovellc.com

Dedicated to:

Mom-for always listening to all of your children and letting us share our joys and sorrows, even to this day

Special acknowledgements:

My family –for your continuous support

Dr. Kimberly Sheppard– for teaching me how to fish

Callie's mom always picked her up from school and asked about her day as soon as she entered the car.

Callie's day at school had been very tough. When her mom asked, "How was your day Callie?" Callie exclaimed, "I had a horrible day Mommy," while stuffing her mouth with grapes, her favorite snack.

Callie went on, "This morning Thomas picked his nose and ate a huge slimy booger." "I yelled out and my teacher made me sit in time out by myself, but I wasn't the one eating my boogers." "It's okay," said Callie's mom after a small chuckle.

Callie sat down to do her homework
while her mom cooked dinner.

However, Callie could not focus on her homework because she wanted to share more about her bad day with her mom.

"In art, that mean girl Meagan stuck her hands in paint and wiped them on the new dress that Grandma bought me," said Callie.

"Oh no sweetie," her mom said in a concerned voice. "I was wondering what happened to your clothes."

"I will try to find another dress and I'll talk to your teacher," said Callie's mom shaking her head. Callie's mom then placed her dinner on the table and told her to eat before it got cold.

Eating dinner reminded Callie
of what happened during lunch.

"Mom," Callie gasped. "By the time I made it through the line there were no pepperoni pizzas left." " I had to eat a boring cheese pizza that looked like a sheet of art paper.

Callie's mom patted her on the back
and took their empty plates to the
kitchen.

While watching her favorite cartoon, Callie remembered what happened to her during reading. Callie knew her mom would be disappointed, but she decided to share anyway.

"In reading," Callie said very slowly, "I forgot the words to my poem and decided to sing my favorite song instead." "My teacher was very upset," said Callie with the saddest look on her face.

"Callie we practiced that poem for two weeks!" her mom groaned.
"I know," Callie said hanging her head. "Mom I was so scared in front of all those people." "I understand," said Callie's mom.

Callie brushed her teeth after her bath and started getting ready for bed.

While brushing her teeth, Callie thought about what happened to her on the playground.

"On the playground I slid down the slide the wrong way and got woodchips in my hair," said Callie. "My classmates called me beaver for the rest of the day." Callie's mom laughed and kissed her on her cheek.

Callie and her mom always read a book before going to bed. After sharing the last story about her day, Callie went to her bookshelf to pick out a book. While choosing a book Callie asked, "How was your day Mom?"

Callie looked over to see that her mom had already fallen fast asleep. "Mom probably had a bad day too," Callie laughed to herself. Callie read her story and fell asleep next to her mom with a smile on her face.

Little Books of Love LLC's Founder Rachel Stubbs makes her authorial debut with *How Was Your Day Mom?* Being a current graduate student pursuing a master's degree in counseling education, Rachel is eager to become an advocate for education. Rachel looks forward to helping children around the world fall in love with literacy with books and supplemental materials. For more information on books and activities from Rachel and Little Books of Love LLC visit: www.littlebooksoflovellc.com

www.ingramcontent.com/pod-product-compliance
Lightning Source LLC
Chambersburg PA
CBHW041610120626
46551CB00002B/383